# If You Plant a Seed

words and paintings by

## KADIR NELSON

Balzer + Bray
*An Imprint of* HarperCollins *Publishers*

If you plant a tomato seed,

a carrot seed,

and a cabbage seed,

in time,

with love and care,

tomato,

carrot,

and cabbage

plants will grow.

If you plant a seed

of selfishness,

in a very short time,

and grow

into a heap

of trouble.

But if you plant

a seed of kindness,

in almost no time at all,

the fruits of kindness

will

grow,

and

grow,

and

grow,

and they are very, very sweet.

For Amel, Aya, and Ali. I love you!

Balzer + Bray is an imprint of HarperCollins Publishers.

If You Plant a Seed

Copyright © 2015 by Kadir Nelson

ISBN 978-0-06-229889-8

The artist painted with oil on canvas to create the illustrations for this book.

Typography by Martha Rago

20 21 RTLO 13 12

❖

First Edition